The
Walker Book of

School Stories

WALKER BOOKS
AND SUBSIDIARIES
LONDON · BOSTON · SYDNEY

D1343998

CONTENTS

BRIAN BIG HEAD

by JEAN URE
illustrated by MIKE GORDON

Esmeralda was starting at her new school, Angel Road Juniors. Esmeralda had been to lots of new schools. This was because she just couldn't resist using her magical powers.

At one school, for instance, she had given the whole class two left feet. ("Because they were so horrid to this poor little boy who was a bit clumsy!")

At another school, she had given the prettiest girl in the class a nose like an old door knocker and made her teeth stick out. ("She was so vain, Mum!")

At yet another, she had turned her class teacher into a wart hog. ("He was really mean! He kept picking on people and making them cry.")

Esmeralda's teacher at Angel Road was called Miss Dainty.

"I won't turn *her* into a wart hog," said Esmeralda, earnestly.

From now on she was going to behave like a normal schoolgirl.

"I promise!" said Esmeralda.

Esmeralda tried. She tried really hard. But it was just *so-o-o* difficult when you had magical powers.

There was a boy in her class called Brian Biggard. The other children called him Brian Big Head. Esmeralda soon discovered why. Every time Miss Dainty asked a question, Brian's hand shot up and Brian's voice very loudly shouted out the answer before anyone else had a chance.

It was extremely annoying. Esmeralda herself was bursting to answer the questions. But Brian always got in first. The others didn't seem to care. They just sat there like puddings. Didn't even bother to try.

Jenna and Amy said there wasn't any point.

"That Big Head," said Amy. "He knows everything."

They were so used to Brian Big Head answering all the questions that it had made them stupid.

And yet they weren't really stupid! Esmeralda was going to have to take some action here. Put her magical powers to good use!

She turned, and let her eyes bore into the back of Brian's head. Just imagine if lots of little holes appeared and all his brains started leaking out...

A voice spoke sharply in Esmeralda's head. *What are you up to?*

Bother! Esmeralda started, guiltily.

That was the trouble with having a mum with magical powers like Esmeralda's. She could glance into her crystal ball at any moment and catch you doing something you shouldn't. She could even get inside your head and read your thoughts. And Brian Big Head was *still* answering all the questions!

It was so unfair.

"Life is like that," said Jenna.

"You just have to put up with it," said Amy.

But Esmeralda tossed her head. Amy and Jenna might put up with it. She wasn't going to!

Esmeralda's mum, Madame Petulengro, was going up to town for the day. And guess what? She was leaving her crystal ball behind!

That meant that she couldn't look into it and see what Esmeralda was up to…

This was Esmeralda's chance. The time had come to teach Brian Big Head a thing or two!

She waited until the first lesson after break. And *then…*

Something very strange began to happen.
Brian's head began to swell! It swelled and it
swelled until

it was the size of
a football ...

the size of
a pumpkin ...

the size of a great gas-filled balloon and
growing even bigger!

The rest of the class sat staring in amazement. One or two of them giggled.

The only person who didn't seem to notice was Miss Dainty. Maybe that had something to do with Esmeralda.

"Who can answer question number four?" said Miss Dainty.

"Question number five?"

"Question number six?"

It was time someone else had a go. Esmeralda didn't want to be as big-headed as Brian (who by now was *very* big-headed indeed). She waited.

But nothing happened. Well, go on! thought Esmeralda. What was the matter with these people? She had silenced Brian Big Head for them! Maybe they needed teaching a lesson too...

Slowly, slowly, all around the room, heads started to shrink.

They shrank to grapefruit ...

shrank to tennis balls ...

shrank to hazelnuts ...

shrank to – pin-heads!

Twenty-four children, with heads so tiny they could scarcely be seen.

"Look at Robert!" giggled Jenna. Then she looked at Amy and her jaw dropped. But only by a millimetre, because now she was a pin-head!

Then Amy looked at Jenna, and her eyes grew wide. But only as wide as a micro-dot, because she was a pin-head, too!

They were *all* pin-heads! The whole lot of them.

Except, of course, for Brian. Brian was a *balloon head*.

And still Miss Dainty didn't notice. "Esmeralda?" she beamed.

"Hey, deary me! How tired I be," sighed Madame Petulengro.

Now there was going to be trouble! Madame Petulengro had come home! *Early*.

She yawned and pulled the crystal ball towards her. What was this she saw? A class full of children with tiny heads (all except for one boy, who had a head like a giant puff ball). And in the midst of them, grinning triumphantly...

Esmeralda!

Drat that girl! She was up to her tricks again.

"*You come home this instant!*" shrieked Madame Petulengro. "*And put those children back the way you found them!*"

"Oh, if I must," sighed Esmeralda.

Miss Dainty turned from the board. She looked across with a smile to where Esmeralda had been sitting.

"Three times seventeen. Es—"

Her voice faded. She looked puzzled. Which child had she been going to ask? Her eye fell on a small rabbity-faced girl sucking her thumb.

"Esther?" said Miss Dainty.

And Esther, who hadn't answered a question for so long that no one could remember, took her thumb out of her mouth and said, "Fifty-one."

Which was, of course, quite correct. Miss Dainty could hardly believe it!

"Question number seven?" she said.

Brian's hand went shooting up. So did Esther's. So did Amy's. So did Jenna's, so did Robert's, so did Jonathan's. So did everyone's!

Miss Dainty blinked. Something very strange was going on in her class.

Yes! Thanks to Esmeralda and her magical powers, they had all woken up from a deep, deep sleep.

TEN PAST TWO

by SAM McBRATNEY
illustrated by IVAN BATES

It wasn't much fun sitting beside Billy Weasel in Crack Willow Wood School.

On Monday he stole little Harvey Stoat's lunch and ate every bit of it. On Tuesday he sharpened Harvey's new pencil at both ends, and this was a thing Harvey never did with his pencils, he only sharpened them at one end. On Wednesday Billy Weasel put Harvey's shoe in the water tub to see if it would float like a boat.

The shoe filled up with water, and sank.

"Look at that shoe!" said Miss Findlay. "It looks like a ship at the bottom of the sea. How can you be so careless with your things, Harvey Stoat?"

Harvey tried to tell her that Billy Weasel had put the shoe in the water, but Miss Findlay hadn't time to listen. His foot was still wet when he got home, so his mother had something to say, too.

"How did that happen?" said Mrs Stoat. "What were you doing with that foot to get it soaking wet like that?"

"Billy Weasel did it and I don't like school any more and I'm not going back," said Harvey.

He spoke quite loudly. Mr and Mrs Stoat could see that Harvey meant what he said.

"Everybody goes to school," said Mr Stoat. "Your friends Hog and Charity go to school. Every word you learn there is like money in the bank, so let us have no more nonsense and silly talk, Young Stoat. Of course you must go to school."

Harvey wasn't happy. As he lay in bed that night the village clock chimed seven times in the distance. "How lovely it would be," he said to himself, "if the time was always seven o'clock. Then I wouldn't have to go to school any more and I wouldn't have to sit beside Billy Weasel."

When the morning came, Harvey brought a rope to school with him. Everyone asked him what the rope was for, but he wouldn't tell them.

"Are you going to climb a mountain?" asked Hog.

"Are you going to play skipping?" asked

Charity Rabbit, who was a very fine skipper.

"He's going to tie up Miss Findlay!" laughed Billy Weasel.

I would like to tie you up, Harvey thought as he glared at Billy Weasel. Instead he added mysteriously, "Wait until ten past two. Then you will see what I am going to do with this rope."

When the village clock struck two, Miss Findlay said goodbye to her class and sent them all home.

At five minutes past two, Harvey climbed up the tower to the village clock with the rope around his shoulders. His friends were amazed to see this happen.

"What is he doing up there?" asked Olivia Vole. The sky was so bright above that she could not see clearly.

"He's unwinding the rope," said Badger. "By Jove, I do believe he's tying up the clock!"

This was a good guess. Far above all their heads, Harvey tied the big hand of the clock to the small one. Now he wound the rope two times around the tower so that the hands could never move. Then he came down again.

"You've stopped the village clock!" said Olivia Vole. "That is the most important clock in the world. How will we know what time it is?"

"Everybody will know what time it is," said Harvey. "It will always be ten past two in the afternoon."

No one knew what to think about this, so there was a long silence. Badger looked at Hog, and Hog looked at Charity Rabbit, who said, "But what about school? If it's always ten past two there can't be any school."

"I know," said Harvey. "They'll have to close it down."

Almost everyone who was there that day could see what a wonderful thing Harvey Stoat had just done. No more school! He had turned every day into a holiday. Billy Weasel was so pleased that he ate his jotter – a thing he had always wanted to do.

Bedtime arrived. Harvey said that he wasn't going to bed because it was still only ten past two in the afternoon. "I tied up the clock with my rope," he explained. "That's how I know what time it is."

Mrs Stoat hurried Harvey into his pyjamas. "I never heard anything so silly," she said to him crossly. "No bedtime, indeed! Look how it's getting dark outside. You can't stop the sun going down at night or coming up in the morning no matter how many clocks you tie up. And you might have fallen down that great big tower and broken your silly leg."

In the morning, Harvey Stoat set off for school with his friends, as usual.

"That was a good idea you had yesterday,

Stoaty," said Hog. "It's a pity it didn't work."

"Oh, I don't know," said Charity Rabbit. "I quite like school."

That's because you don't sit beside Billy Weasel, thought Harvey.

Before long Miss Findlay asked them to set out their jotters on the table for some work with numbers. Everyone did so except for Billy Weasel.

"And where is *your* jotter?" Miss Findlay asked him.

"Billy Weasel ate his jotter yesterday, Miss," said Hog.

"He ate his jotter? He ate his good jotter? How much of it did he eat?"

"All of it," Badger called out.

There was quite a bit of laughing at that, but Billy Weasel didn't think it was funny when Miss Findlay made him sit on his own at the Silly Table.

"And you will sit there until you learn that jotters are not to be eaten like sweets!" she cried.

Harvey felt a little sorry for Billy Weasel, sitting over at the Silly Table without a friend close by. Then he remembered his wet shoe, and did his very best writing with a new pencil sharpened only at one end.

THE SUPER-DOODLE PLAN

by **VIVIAN FRENCH**
illustrated by **THELMA LAMBERT**

"I wish we'd never moved house," Rosie said, crunching her toast in a gloomy sort of way. "And I wish we didn't have to go to a new school. I bet all the kids in our form will be *horrible*."

"Yeah – they'll all be seven foot tall," Chris said, "with little piggy eyes. And they'll all be called Basher or Smasher or Grab."

"Or they'll be frilly little girls with drippy curls called Fluffy or Twinkie, who stick rulers in your back when you're not looking. And I bet they lie in wait for new kids and snatch their lunch boxes—"

"And take all their books and tear all the pages out because they can't write even their names and they *hate* anyone who can write—"

"And they catch you at break times and dinner

27

times and shove your head down the toilet…"

Chris looked at Rosie. "Would someone's head get stuck if it was shoved down the toilet?"

Rosie rolled her eyes. "Yeah – stuck for weeks and weeks and weeks. And the school cleaner would only find you when you were a little heap of smelly bones, and she'd sweep you up and say 'Yuck, another nasty school dinner.'"

Chris spread his third piece of bread with peanut butter and jam and honey. "I still don't see why we had to move house anyway," he said with his mouth full. "It was OK at the last place."

"You're a pig," Rosie said. "That's all the honey gone. And I hated our old house. Whoever wants to live with two other families all the time? Squash squash squash, and always someone in the bathroom."

"Mimsie wimsie." Chris made a face. "Rosie Posie wants to do her hair all pretty for the boys."

Rosie picked up the sugar bowl and tipped it over Chris's plate just as Mum came in with the baby.

"*Rosie!*" she said. "*Whatever* are you doing?"

"Nothing," said Rosie.

"That's a horrible waste of sugar," said Mum. "If you're going to throw it about like that you'd better do without your sweets on Saturday."

"But—"

"And if you don't hurry up, you'll be late for school – and it's your first day. Go and get your coats on." Mum sat down with the baby. She had her don't-argue-with-me-or-else face on, and Rosie and Chris pulled their coats down from the hooks in the hall.

"I don't think I feel very well," Chris said.

"Tough," said Mum. "Have you got your lunch boxes?"

"It won't look very good if I'm sick all over everyone on the first day," Chris said hopefully.

Rosie began to take her coat off again. "If Chris is feeling sick, I am too. And don't think I'm going to that horrible school all by myself, because I'm not."

"It's a perfectly ordinary school," Mum said. "Just like your last one."

Chris and Rosie looked at each other. Chris made a *yuck* face, and Rosie crossed her eyes.

"And anyway," Mum went on, "you've got just ten minutes to get there. I showed you the way yesterday, and Mrs Bettinson is expecting you. *Now – go!*"

Chris and Rosie picked up their lunch boxes.

They did up their coats and walked slowly to the door. Mum followed them as far as the gate.

"Have a lovely day," she said. "I'm sure you'll make friends with lots of children – and Freddie and I'll be waiting to hear all about it."

She blew them two kisses and went back inside. Freddie smiled at them over Mum's shoulder as she carried him in.

"It's all right for babies," said Chris as they began trailing slowly down the road. "All they have to do is sit around and eat and sleep. It's us that have to do all the nasty things."

"Yeah – and watch out for Smasher and Basher and Grab," said Rosie.

"Most mums would take their children to school and protect them from attack," Chris said grumpily. "Just because we've got a baby we're stuck on our own."

"Well..." Rosie was looking thoughtful. "At least we don't have Mum fussing and telling Mrs what's-her-name what good little twinnies we are."

"Are we?" asked Chris. "We're not usually."

"Idiot." Rosie stopped walking and leant against the fence. "Listen – no one knows anything about us, right?"

"Right."

"They just know that two new kids — twins — are coming to the school. Right?"

"Right."

"So they don't know if we're any good at anything. We could be Martians for all they know."

"Yes?"

"Well — why don't we pretend that one of us can't speak, and the other one can't hear?"

Chris looked puzzled. Sometimes Rosie's plans weren't very straightforward. "Why?" he asked.

Rosie pushed him. "Because," she said, "then we won't have to do any work — and if anyone tries to bully us the teacher will stop them."

Chris opened and shut his mouth. "OK," he said. "But couldn't we be Martians instead?"

"No," said Rosie firmly. "And bags I be the one who can't talk. You'll have to tell them what I'm saying. You can understand me, but no one else can. Uggga ummmm gagagaga…"

"What does that mean?" Chris asked.

Rosie looked at him. "Hm," she said. "Actually, I think you'd better be the one who can't talk. Can you make noises?"

"Urgle urgle ooop ooop," said Chris. "Yorooo yorooo." He threw his lunch box up in the air and caught it. "Yacky yacky! It's a super-doodle plan,

Rosie – ziffy diffy niffy!" He collapsed in giggles against a lamppost.

Rosie caught at his arm and shook it.

"Sh!" she said. "There's some other children coming – we'd better go!"

"Nummy nummy," Chris said cheerfully, and they began to hurry along the road.

All the rest of the way to the school gates they kept close together and didn't look at any of the other children rushing and pushing and shoving along the pavement with them. Chris muttered "Oooogle dooogle" to himself when a bigger boy bumped into him, but Rosie said "Sshh!" fiercely. The bigger boy looked back and said "Sorry" in quite a friendly way, but Rosie glared at him and he went on.

The bell went just as they reached the gates. There was a mad stampede, and children flooded through the open front doors. Rosie and Chris were left standing outside, together with a small girl with wildly curling black hair and spectacles.

"Hullo," she said. "Are you new too?"

"Voop voop voop," said Chris cheerfully. Rosie pinched his arm, but he took no notice. "B'rrrm b'rrrrm," he added.

The girl looked puzzled. "Is that a joke?" she asked.

Rosie put on her most serious face. "This is poor brother," she said, in a strange squeak. "He no speak. I no hear. You shout when you talk to me."

The girl stared at her for a moment, and then said in a very angry voice, "I s'pose you think you're funny, but I think you're real nerds. Shove off." And she pushed past them. "I'll find my own way in, and I hope I never ever see you again." She stumped in through the school doors.

"Oh," Chris said. "She's gone."

Rosie was feeling uncomfortable. She wasn't certain, but she thought the girl had been just about to cry.

"Huh," she said, pretending she didn't care. "She's just exactly what I knew we'd find here."

"I thought she looked quite nice," said Chris.

"*Yuck!*" Rosie said loudly. "You *must* be joking."

"Oi!" Someone was standing in the school door. It was the tall boy who had pushed against them on the way to school. "Are you twins? Are you called Winter?"

"Yes," said Chris, and then clapped his hand to his mouth. "I mean – dilly dilly dilly."

"Is he mad?" the tall boy asked Rosie.

Rosie put her special face back on. "This my brother Chris Winter. He no speak, I no hear. Please talk loud."

The boy nodded, and grinned. Then he shouted at the top of his voice, "YOU'VE GOT TO COME WITH ME 'COS YOU'RE IN MY CLASS WITH MRS BETTINSON. OH, MY NAME'S GARY."

Rosie tried to look as if she was having difficulty understanding, although her ears were ringing.

"Why you scary?" she squeaked.

The tall boy leant towards her, and bellowed so loudly in her ear that she jumped.

"MY ... NAME ... IS ... GARY!"

"Hoodly hoodly hoodly," said Chris, who was feeling left out of the conversation.

"Twiddly twiddly twiddly," said Gary, and he led them along a corridor full of coats and shoebags and lunch boxes.

"YOU PUT YOUR COATS HERE!" he shouted, pointing at the pegs. "SHALL I HELP YOU?"

"We're not daft," said Rosie crossly. She took off her coat and hung it up. Chris took his off as well, and Gary carefully arranged it for him on a peg near Rosie's.

"WHAT'S YOUR NAME?" Gary roared at Rosie.

Rosie shook her head. She was beginning to feel that she might really be going deaf. Her head was hurting – but she didn't want to give up. Not yet, anyway.

"Boffy moffy toffy," Chris said. He was wondering if Gary liked football, and how he was ever going to find out.

"YOU'RE CALLED BOFFY?" Gary grinned at Rosie more than ever. "CHRIS AND BOFFY. THAT'S NICE FOR YOU."

A door in the corridor opened, and a teacher's head popped out.

"Whatever's going on out here? Oh it's you, Gary. I might have guessed. Couldn't you just *try* and be quieter?"

"Morning, Mr Patel," said Gary. "I'm just taking these new kids to their form, and one of them's deaf."

"You should be taking him to the unit, then," said Mr Patel, and he popped back into his classroom.

"HE'S RIGHT, YOU KNOW," said Gary. He

turned round and took Rosie's sleeve. "COME ON, BOFFY. WE'D BETTER TAKE YOU TO THE UNIT."

Rosie began to feel worried. What was a unit?

"Me see Mrs Bettinson," she squeaked.

"OH, NO." Gary took her firmly by the arm. "THIS WAY."

Chris thought it was time he helped out.

"Upple dupple!" he said, and pointed back along the way they had been heading. "Boffy? Boffy Chris?"

"Just a minute, Chris," Gary said. "We'll dump Boffy in the unit, and then we'll go back to class. Hey – can you play football?"

Chris nodded excitedly. "Footie footie footie!"

"Great. Oh – this is the unit. I mean, THIS IS THE UNIT! DEAF AND PARTIALLY-HEARING KIDS THIS WAY!" Gary swung Rosie round a sharp corner and opened a glass door. Rosie saw an ordinary-looking classroom, with several children sitting at tables. A tall thin woman was bending over a girl, and Rosie recognized the curly-haired girl who had met them at the school entrance.

Bother, Rosie thought. She won't want to see me.

The teacher looked up. "Hullo, Gary. What are you doing here?"

"Brought you a new girl, Mrs Clark. Her name's Boffy. ISN'T IT, BOFFY?" Gary bent down to shriek into Rosie's ear.

"Are you sure?" Mrs Clark picked up a piece of paper from her desk. "I was expecting Harindar, and she's here safely — but no one said anything about anyone else."

The dark-haired girl caught Rosie's eye. To Rosie's amazement she looked very surprised, and then smiled and patted the seat beside her.

"Well — she can stay for the moment," said Mrs Clark. "Thank you, Gary. You'd better run along now. Is that Boffy's brother?"

"Yeah — he can hear all right, though. He's just mad," said Gary cheerfully. "Come on, Chris." And to Rosie's horror the two of them hurried out of the room and slammed the door behind them.

"Just sit down for now, Boffy dear," said Mrs Clark. "I see you and Harindar know each other — you'd better sit next to her. Now, is everyone looking and listening? Right. Then get on with your work, and I'll just pop out and see if I can find out who should be here and who shouldn't."

Rosie sat down beside the dark-haired girl. She

was feeling quite desperate. Here she was in a strange room, in a strange school, and her head was ringing with the sound of Gary's amazingly loud voice. Chris had gone off and left her without a backward glance — and he might do or say anything when she wasn't around to keep an eye on him.

Harindar touched her arm. Rosie looked at her, wondering why she was suddenly being friendly. Harindar's mouth was moving, and Rosie realized that she was saying something. She was saying something — but Rosie couldn't hear a word. Help! thought Rosie. It's all the fault of that horrible Gary — he's made me really not able to hear anything. And I'll never be the same again... To her horror, Rosie found that she wanted to cry. She *never* cried, but now her eyes were filling, and her throat felt tight and sore. She gave a sort of cough, and stared hard at her table-top.

Harindar pulled gently at her sleeve. Rosie saw that she was passing her a note.

> Is your name rarely Boffin?
> R you OK? Sory I was cros-
> I thort you were larffing at me.
> Peple do lots, but I can heer if
> you talk at me and look at me.
> I lip reed — don't you?
>   Im calld Harrie

Rosie read the note twice. Then she swallowed and looked at Harrie. Could she really understand just people's lips moving? Harrie must be terribly clever, Rosie thought. Much cleverer than she was.

Rosie leant forward. "I'm called Rosie. Can you really tell what I'm saying?" she mouthed.

Harrie nodded, her eyes twinkling. "Of course," she whispered. "Do you sign?"

Rosie looked blank. "Sign?"

Harrie shook her head. "Dear me," she whispered. "No wonder you're here."

"But what do you mean?"

"Like that —" Harrie pointed to where a group of children at the back of the class were giggling in a secret sort of way. They were moving their hands and arms about, and Rosie realized that they were understanding each other through the signs that they were making.

"That is *so* clever," Rosie said, watching. "Does it take long to learn?"

Harrie was looking at her in a puzzled sort of way. "Did you say something?"

Rosie turned towards her. "Could I learn to do that? What does it mean? It's lovely!"

Harrie pulled a face. "I can't do it – well, only bits. I have quite a lot of hearing, so I never learnt. This means 'pig', though." She scrunched up her hand into a fist and circled it in front of her nose. "Pig pig pig."

"Wow! We could have whole conversations, and no one would hear us!" Rosie was cheering up fast.

Harrie touched Rosie's hand. "You must look at me – I can't see what you're saying."

Rosie gasped. "Oh, I'm sorry. I'm just not used to it. I've never met a deaf person before. Well – apart from my gran, and I just shout at her. You're *much* cleverer."

Harrie had a strange look on her face. She bit her lip and then shook her head. "You're not deaf, are you?" she said. "You can hear just like ordinary people."

There was a long silence, and Rosie felt herself go very red. She faced Harrie and said, "I'm ever so sorry. I was pretending. I didn't want to go to a new school, and I thought if I said I couldn't hear it'd be more fun. I didn't mean to make fun of you – I really truly didn't."

Harrie didn't say anything for a moment. Then she began to laugh. "However are you going to tell Mrs Lark?" she said.

"Mrs Clark?" Rosie rubbed her nose. "I don't know. Do you think she'd believe me if I said I was *sometimes* deaf?"

"No," said Harrie, "I don't."

The door opened, and Mrs Clark came in. Rosie and Harrie looked at each other, and Harrie made a face.

"Is there a girl here called Rosie Winter?" Mrs Clark asked.

Rosie shuffled her feet and put her hand up.

Mrs Clark blinked, and peered at her. "I thought you were called Boffy, dear?"

Rosie shook her head.

Mrs Clark looked cross. "Is there some foolishness going on here? I'm quite sure you said your name was Boffy."

Harrie put her hand up. "Please, Mrs Lark, her

name really is Rosie. It was the boy who came in who said she was Boffy."

Mrs Clark began to laugh. "Of course it was — how silly of me. I should know Gary by now, goodness knows. I'm sorry, Rosie dear. It seems you're in the wrong class, and Harindar is as well."

Harrie sat up straighter and opened her eyes wide.

Mrs Clark moved to stand in front of her. "We understood you didn't know anyone else here, dear, so we thought we'd start you in the unit. Now we know you know Rosie, it's rather different. We wondered if perhaps you'd like to see how you get on in a mixed ability class together?"

Harrie turned to Rosie. She looked as if she wasn't quite certain what to say. Rosie smiled her widest smile and mouthed, "Say yes! *Please* say yes!"

Harrie turned to Mrs Clark. "Yes please," she said. "I'd like that."

"That's all right then," Mrs Clark said cheerfully. "It's much nicer to be with your friends. Now, run along. Mrs Bettinson said she'd send someone down to show you the way. And I hope you'll pop in here and see us sometimes. Most children do."

Harrie and Rosie said goodbye and went out into the corridor. Gary was leaning against the wall, grinning.

"HI, BOFFY!" he shouted. "STILL FINDING IT HARD TO HEAR? CHRIS SAYS YOU CAN HEAR OK EXCEPT ON THE FIRST DAY OF SCHOOL!"

Rosie glared at him. Just wait till I see Chris, she thought. Suddenly she remembered something. She made her hand into a fist and circled it in front of her nose. She looked at Harrie, and Harrie nodded. They both began to laugh.

Gary stopped grinning and stared at them. "What's the joke?" he asked.

"Tell you sometime," Rosie said. "We'll tell you sometime when you're being very, very quiet..." And she and Harrie smiled at each other as they followed Gary along the corridor that led to Mrs Bettinson's room.

POSH WATSON

by GILLIAN CROSS
illustrated by MIKE GORDON

Crumble Lane School was dull. Not just a bit dull, like other schools, but so dull that even the spiders on the ceilings yawned.

The school uniform was grey, the classrooms were cold and bare, and all the teachers were as dull as dust. Especially Mrs Juniper, the Head. Her voice was so boring that everyone yawned every time she spoke.

The only person who was happy at Crumble Lane was Natalie. That was because she never took any notice of Mrs Juniper. She didn't care about the teachers either, or the classrooms. She spent her whole time sitting with a heap of maths sheets, working away as hard as she could. She liked maths better than anything else in the world.

And every time she finished a sheet, her teacher took it away and stuck it up on the wall, as a decoration.

That's how boring Crumble Lane was.

One dull Monday morning, Natalie was tying her grey school tie round the neck of her grey shirt when there was a knock on the door.

She opened the door – and almost fainted.

Outside was a boy in a purple jacket. He was wearing giant sunglasses and his hair stuck out all round his head, in bright yellow spikes.

He waved his lunch box at her. It was gold, and his initials sparkled in diamonds on the side.

"Hi, I'm Posh Watson," he said, "your new next-door neighbour."

Natalie picked up her grey school coat, kissed her dad goodbye and stepped outside. "All right. Follow me," she said.

But Posh wasn't much good at following. For most of the way he was ahead of her, turning cartwheels along the pavement and waving at everyone in grey uniform. By the time they reached the school gates, there were twenty children following, all with their mouths open.

Mrs Juniper was standing in the playground with the bell in her hand. When she saw Posh, she almost dropped it. *Her* mouth fell open.

Posh cartwheeled straight up to her.

"Hi!" he said. "I'm Posh Watson. It's great to be here. Fan-doodle-tastic!"

"I – er –" Mrs Juniper didn't know what to say. "Good morning." Posh yawned. But Mrs Juniper didn't even notice. People always yawned when she spoke.

She rang the bell – and Posh stood on his hands and waggled his feet in her face.

"Hoo-doodle-ray," he said. "Let's get inside and start the fun!"

Natalie had a dreadful day. Whenever she tried to settle down with her maths sheets, people came up and poked her in the ribs.

All the children knew she was Posh's neighbour, and they thought she knew everything about him. They wouldn't leave her alone – even when she pulled faces and growled at them – because they wanted clothes like his.

Silly idiots. Fancy wanting to copy him! He's mad, thought Natalie.

By Tuesday, everyone else seemed to be mad too. When Natalie got to school, the playground was full of peculiar clothes.

And everyone was yelling strange words.

Natalie stood and stared. She seemed to be the only person in ordinary school uniform. Everyone else was trying to be Posh Watson. She looked round for the real Posh, to see what he thought about it all.

But he wasn't there. Even when Mrs Juniper came out to ring the bell, there was no sign of him.

Or was there?

Suddenly, a Rolls-Royce drew up outside the school and a very strange person stepped out of the back. He was wearing a long cloak and a black hat was pulled down over his hair. He came slinking through the gates and over to Natalie, just as Mrs Juniper rang the bell.

The strange person swept off his hat. It was Posh all right, but he looked quite, quite different.

Natalie blinked. "W-where's your purple jacket? And what about the spikes in your hair?"

"Do me a *favour*." Posh looked at her, crushingly. "Spikes are out. Only bondos have spikes in their hair now."

"B-bondos?" Natalie said.

"That's right." Posh waved a hand scornfully round the playground. "Only bondos are still wearing spikes and purple jackets."

Mrs Juniper rang the bell again, and Posh stalked into school, leaving everyone else muttering behind him.

Natalie sighed. Today was going to be even worse than yesterday. She'd be lucky if she got any work done.

She was right. The moment she sat down in her corner at the back of the class, people began to creep up to her.

Mrs Juniper wasn't very happy, either. When they left school that afternoon, they found a notice stuck up on the school gate.

NO purple coats!
NO spiked hair!
BY ORDER
J. Juniper

There weren't any purple coats or spiked hair at school on Wednesday, but lots of people came in black cloaks and hats with feathers. The feathers got tangled up, and the cloaks kept knocking things over and catching on splinters.

Natalie thought it was all Posh's fault. But she couldn't say anything because he wasn't there.

He didn't get to school until playtime. And when he did, he wasn't wearing a black cloak, or a hat with a feather.

He came marching into the playground in a pair of huge pink trainers that played trumpet music whenever he took a step.

And he wouldn't say anything except:

Boom-ba-boom!

NO CLOAKS OR FEATHERS by order J. Juniper

On Thursday, Posh was there early. When Natalie arrived, he was lying in the middle of the playground doing press-ups, in a T-shirt and a pair of running shorts. He had bare feet.

Natalie glared at him.

"Why aren't you wearing your trumpet-trainers?" she said crossly. "Everyone else is."

Posh jumped up and did a back flip. "Exactly! Musical shoes are glazzed-out."

"Glazzed-out?" Natalie said.

"Glazzed right out," said Posh. "They're not whirrabubble."

Natalie groaned. She was having a dreadful week. By that afternoon, she'd done only two and a half maths sheets, and the teacher didn't put those on the wall. All kinds of other things kept getting stuck up instead.

Whenever Natalie settled down to work, people flicked notes at her and hissed in her ear.

People kept trying to find out what Posh was going to do *next*, so that they wouldn't get left behind. And they all thought Natalie knew, because she was his neighbour.

She was having a miserable time.

So was Mrs Juniper.

On Friday morning, Natalie and Posh walked to school together. As they reached the gates, someone pushed a note under Posh's nose.

Natalie looked at him. He was wearing a long earring, with a packet of chewing gum on the end, and a false moustache.

"Well... You've got to go," she said.

Natalie dragged Posh up the corridor to Mrs Juniper's office, knocked on the door and pushed him in. He was still cross, and he grabbed hold of her arm and pulled her in too.

Mrs Juniper looked at Posh. She looked at the earring and the chewing gum and the moustache. And she frowned.

"The Inspectors are coming on Monday," she said. "Everyone's *got* to wear uniform."

She wrote a new notice.

Then she thought again, and wrote another one.

When she'd done that, she looked severely at Posh. "On Monday, I want to see you in a proper school uniform. Like Natalie."

"Like Natalie?" Posh looked at her and his eyes widened. "You mean – you want me to wear a skirt?"

"Of course not!" Mrs Juniper snapped. "I want you to wear Proper School Uniform. Like – like that." She pointed at last year's school photograph which was stuck up on her wall.

Posh stared at the rows of children in neat, tidy uniform.

I can't wear clothes like that!

Why not?

They're dull!

"But if you don't wear them, nobody else will," Mrs Juniper said. "There will be terrible trouble when the Inspectors come."

"I don't care about trouble," Posh said. "And I've got a really whizzaceous idea for Monday."

Mrs Juniper looked as if she were going to faint. "But everyone will copy you!"

"I like people copying me," Posh said.

Oh, dear! thought Natalie — and that was when she had her brainwave.

She looked at Mrs Juniper. She looked at Posh. She thought about the Inspectors. Then, in a very small voice, she said, "I've got a *really* whizzaceous idea. If you do what I say, you can both have what you want..."

On Monday, Natalie got up early. She dressed as usual, in her school uniform — grey skirt, grey shirt, grey tie.

Want to know what Posh is wearing today?

Then she ran downstairs and phoned Samantha, the school gossip.

Then she had her breakfast and walked to school with her fingers crossed.

At five to nine, the Inspectors arrived in their big black cars. They looked out over the playground. All the children were in neat school uniform. Even Posh Watson.

The Inspectors yawned.

Natalie went up to them.

Shall I take you into assembly?

The Inspectors nodded, and yawned even harder. Natalie knew just what they were thinking. *This school is even duller than last time we came.* She crossed her fingers again and led them into the hall.

They sat up on the platform, yawning as the children walked in.

They looked very bored.

When all the children were sitting down, there was a most extraordinary noise at the back of the hall.

And in came the teachers!

Every teacher was wearing something wild and strange and weird. And behind them all, dancing and prancing up the middle of the hall, came someone Natalie hardly recognized – *Mrs Juniper!*

She bounded onto the stage, beamed at the Inspectors and held out her hand.

"Hi, bondos! I'm Mrs Jumping Juniper! Welcome to Crumble Lane!"

The Inspectors sat up straight and their eyes opened wide. They weren't yawning any more.

And they didn't yawn when Mrs Juniper showed them round the school.

They were too busy looking at the pictures on the walls.

At the neat, tidy children.

And the wild, weird teachers.

And the amazing, energetic Head – Mrs Jumping Juniper.

Mrs Jumping Juniper was so happy she was actually smiling. She'd got what she wanted at last.

Posh was smiling too. Because everyone had copied him now – even the teachers.

But the happiest person in the whole school was sitting in a corner all by herself. Nobody was bothering her –

and she was having a wonderful time.

MAGIC IN THE AIR

by JUNE CREBBIN
illustrated by THELMA LAMBERT

WELCOME TO BOOK WEEK said the notice on Carrie's school door. Every day there were book puzzles and quizzes, competitions and special events.

Carrie loved it all. She enjoyed listening to stories and poems. She had saved up her pocket money to buy a book at the Book Sale. But most of all she was looking forward to Friday.

Friday was Dressing-up Day, when everyone could come to school dressed as a character from a book. Mrs Taylor said they could stay in their costumes all day, even through dinner time. In the morning there would be a parade in the hall and a competition to guess the names of the characters. Carrie was going to be Alice in Wonderland. David was having problems.

"Has your mum changed her mind?" said Carrie at home-time on Thursday. "Is she going to let you be the Saucepan Man?"

"No," said David. "She still thinks it's too noisy. She says Mrs Taylor won't want me banging and crashing about all day in a pile of saucepans."

Carrie giggled. "Mrs Taylor would have to put her earplugs in!"

Everyone was rushing past them out of school. Carrie and David walked down the path to the school gates.

"But who *are* you going to come as?" said Carrie.

"I wish I knew," said David.

Poor David. It would be dreadful if he were the only person not dressed up. "I hope you will think of someone," Carrie said.

"My mum will," said David. "She promised she'd think of someone today."

Carrie caught sight of Dad waving to her.

"I have to go now," she said. "See you tomorrow – whoever you are!"

She edged her way through the mass of parents, children and pushchairs to where Dad was waiting.

"Dressing-up Day tomorrow," she said as they set off for home. "I can't wait. Guess who I'm going to be."

"I don't know," said Dad. "Give me some clues."

"I'll be wearing my bridesmaid's dress," said Carrie, "and my hair will be loose so that I can wear an Alice-band..." She paused and looked meaningfully at Dad.

"I get it," he said. "So-called because Alice in Wonderland used to wear one."

"Yes!" said Carrie. "Do you think they'll get it tomorrow at school? I'm going to carry a little bottle with DRINK ME on the label."

"Then I definitely think they'll get it," said Dad.

"Good," said Carrie. They turned in at the gate. "Tonight," she said, "Mum's going to get my dress out of the attic and iron it. I'm going to make the DRINK ME label and you can stick it on my little green perfume bottle."

"Thank you," said Dad.

After tea, Mum went up the ladder into the attic.

"Can I come?" called Carrie.

"Better not," said Mum. "I'll be down in a minute."

She appeared again almost immediately and came down backwards with a flat square box. "Here it is."

Carrie lifted the blue dress out of the tissue paper. "It'll be just right," said Mum, popping it over Carrie's head, "with your white lacy tights and black patent shoes. What's the matter?"

"It hurts my arms," said Carrie.

"Oh dear," said Mum, standing back to look at her. "The sleeves are far too tight."

"It's all too tight," said Carrie. "I can't breathe properly." She went to look in the mirror. "And it's too short." She was close to tears. "It's all wrong."

"Perhaps I could let it out a bit," said Mum, easing the dress over Carrie's head to look at the seams.

"Can you?" said Carrie. She sat on the bed, shivering.

Mum shook her head. "I'm afraid there isn't any spare material. I'm so sorry, Carrie. I should have realized you'd have grown out of it by now. Pop your jumper and skirt back on and come downstairs. We'll have to think of something else."

"But we haven't got anything else," said Carrie. She thought of David. It would be awful if neither of them was dressed up.

"We'll think of something," said Mum.

While Dad put Amy to bed, Mum and Carrie looked through the dressing-up box.

"What about Red Riding Hood?" said Carrie. "We could make a cape out of a red velvet curtain."

But there was only a pair of blue velvet curtains in the box. And they were old. Everything was old.

"Let's look through your books," said Mum. "They'll give us some ideas. We'll make a list." They wrote down Snow White, the Wicked Witch and the Queen of Hearts. Finding characters was easy – thinking how to dress them was the difficult bit.

When Dad came down he tried to help too. "What about your dressing-up clothes?" he said.

"We've tried that," said Carrie. "They're too old."

She sat on the carpet and opened *Tales from Many Lands*.

"We've thought of lots of characters," said Mum, showing Dad the list. "But we can't think how to dress them."

Carrie turned the pages. She stopped at a picture of a boy wearing trousers the colour of a summer sky. His jacket was blue to match and beautifully embroidered with tiny red and gold dragons. They pranced across the front and round the sleeves and even along the little stand-up collar.

Carrie jumped up in excitement.

"Found something?" said Dad.

"I think so," said Carrie and ran upstairs.

When she came down, she was wearing the blue

pyjamas that Dad had brought her – her present from China.

"Look," she said, "and look at the picture."

Mum and Dad looked. They looked from the picture to Carrie and back to the picture.

"Aladdin!" said Dad. "As I live and breathe. I remember you said those pyjamas were too beautiful to sleep in..."

"But just right for Aladdin." Carrie smiled.

Mum agreed. "You'll need a hat," she said. "Like the one in the picture." She fetched some cardboard and glue and set to work.

"You'll need an enchanted lamp," said Dad, who was on his knees studying the picture.

"No, I won't," said Carrie. "Aladdin doesn't *have* to have a lamp." She knew there were no enchanted lamps lying around the house.

"Well, we shall see," said Dad.

Carrie went off to have her bath. Afterwards she tried on her costume. Mum plaited her hair and popped on the hat. It fitted perfectly.

"And now," said Dad, "for the thing Aladdin couldn't do without." From behind his back, he produced – a lamp!

It was beautiful, just the right shape and size. Carrie held it carefully.

"Where did you get it?" she said.

Dad parted the silver paper covering, so that Carrie could peep underneath. She giggled. "It's our gravy jug!"

"*Was* our gravy jug," said Dad. "Now it's Aladdin's magic lamp."

"Magic?" said Carrie.

"Definitely," said Dad. "So just be careful. You never know what might happen."

Carrie was so excited. Everything was coming right again. As she fell asleep, she thought a little of David. But in her dreams she was already Aladdin, polishing the lamp to summon a mighty genie. "What is your wish, O Master?" said the Genie, bowing low before her. "I am the Slave of the Lamp."

Next morning in the playground, Carrie noticed there were three Alice in Wonderlands but no one else was Aladdin. She looked for David. Witches and fairies, pirates and outlaws, scarecrows and even a lion were swarming about the playground. But David wasn't any of them. He still wasn't there when the bell went and they all had to go inside.

"Goodness!" said Mrs Taylor as everyone came in. "There must be magic in the air. I was expecting my class today but all these people have turned up instead."

They sat on the carpet and tried to make themselves comfortable. But there wasn't as much room as usual. Red Riding Hood sat on a sword by mistake and began to cry. Mrs Taylor comforted her. "I tell you what," she said to everyone, "why don't we put all your special things on this table to keep them safe until it's time for the parade."

So all the swords, bows and arrows, wands, shepherds' crooks, DRINK ME bottles and the magic lamp were put safely in a corner of the classroom.

"That's better," said Mrs Taylor. She began to call the register.

"Rupert Bear?"

"Yes, Mrs Taylor."

"Little Bo Peep? ... The Queen of Hearts? ... Jack Horner?" Everyone answered in their turn. Three people answered to Alice in Wonderland. Carrie remembered to answer to Aladdin but she was thinking about David. She wished he was there. It wasn't the same without him.

"Only one missing," said Mrs Taylor as she closed the register. "What a shame. Never mind. He may turn up later." She gazed around the room. "I wonder," she said, "who can come and show us a bit about their character? Come on, Bo Peep. Come and show us how you lost your sheep."

Bo Peep fetched her crook and stood at the front of the class. She put up her hand to shade her eyes. She looked one way and then the other.

"Lovely," said Mrs Taylor and she began to sing, "Little Bo Peep has lost her sheep..." and everyone joined in. Bo Peep did some more looking and then sat down while everyone clapped.

Cinderella swept the floor vigorously with her broom. The Mad Hatter and all three Alices sat down to have tea, and the Queen of Hearts strutted up and down with her tray of jam tarts, promising everyone they could have one at playtime. Then Incy Wincy Spider tried to climb up the spout, or at least onto a table and then onto a chair and then onto a cupboard – but the chair wobbled a bit so Mrs Taylor said the sun had come out and it was time for him to come down.

"Well," said Mrs Taylor eventually, looking round, "who hasn't had a turn? Aladdin? Come on, Aladdin. Come and show us how you polish your magic lamp."

Aladdin fetched the lamp from the table and stood in front of the class. Everyone watched. Aladdin rubbed the lamp with his sleeve...

The door flew open and in came a genie!

Everyone gasped, even Aladdin.

The Genie was dressed in the richest colours —
his crimson waistcoat trimmed with gold, his
baggy trousers shining with sequins, and on his
head a gold turban with a dazzling jewel at the
centre.

"It's magic," said Robin Hood.

And before the Genie could say "What is your
wish, O Master? I am the Slave of the Lamp",
everyone clapped and cheered and clapped some
more.

"Well," said Mrs Taylor as the Genie and
Aladdin sat down together on the carpet. "Now
we're *all* here. What a good job Aladdin came to
school today. And we've still time for a story before
the parade. Whose story shall it be?"

"Aladdin and the Genie!" everyone shouted.

So Mrs Taylor began. "Once upon a time, in a far
off city in China, there lived a boy called
Aladdin..."

LADY LONG-LEGS

by JAN MARK
illustrated by PAUL HOWARD

Nisba was a new girl. Everyone else in her class had been at Farm Lane School for three years and one term. Nisba had been there for three days.

It was cold and frosty outside, but the hall was warm and cosy.

After assembly, Nisba said to Mr Martin, "Where does the warm come from?"

"Warmth," Mr Martin said. "Do you know what, Nisba? You are the first person who has ever asked me that."

Mr Martin liked people to ask him questions. He was not so happy when they told him things. They told him things all day long.

"Sir, Neesa's got mud on her shoes."

"Mr Martin, Aishe's taken my crayons."

"Farid's hitting Robert, Sir."

Nisba was new. She had nothing to tell him yet.

"We have under-floor heating," Mr Martin said. "There are hot pipes down there under the floor tiles. That is why the tiles keep coming unstuck. The glue melts and the tiles split."

The floor of the hall was red and black tiles, but in places there were blue tiles instead of black ones, and pink tiles instead of red ones. Mr Keates, the caretaker, never had enough of the right colours when he mended the floor.

And there was one white tile, almost in the middle of the doorway. Nisba had learned one important thing already. It was very bad luck to walk on the white tile.

If someone walked on the white tile they had to stand on one leg and count to twenty, with their fingers crossed. Otherwise they got bad luck.

On the very first day Robert had fallen down the steps in the corridor and broken his arm. Everyone said it was because he walked on the white tile going in to assembly and didn't bother to count to twenty with his fingers crossed.

Robert said it was because Farid had pushed him, but everyone knew about the white tile. Aishe had seen him walk on it.

Nisba was not afraid of the white tile in the hall, so she walked on it. People said that if you stood on a blue tile and a pink tile at the same time, all your teeth would fall out. No one dared to try it.

Mr Keates did it all the time. He had false teeth.

It was different in the corridor. In the corridor the tiles were brown.

"Brown is the colour of footprints," Mr Martin said. "The colour of mud and dust and old, old dinner."

But not all of the tiles were brown. Down the middle of the corridor there was a pattern like a hopscotch grid, made of green and yellow tiles.

They were not allowed to play hopscotch indoors but the patterns were not wasted. Some people would walk only on brown tiles. Some people took big steps and walked only on yellow tiles. The ones with very long legs could get all the way from the front door to the hall on green tiles.

The six steps by the staff room were all brown. They did not count.

Nisba had long legs. On the fourth day of term she went right down the corridor on green tiles, but as she passed the cloakroom a big girl came out. It was Lucy Wells.

"You can't do that," Lucy said. "It's not allowed."

"What isn't?" Nisba said.

"Only people in Year 4 can walk on green tiles," Lucy said.

Nisba looked at Lucy. "What year are you in?"

"Year 4," Lucy said. "You're not in Year 4."

Nisba took a big step from one green tile to the next.

Lucy stamped. "You can't do that!"

"Yes I can," Nisba said, and took another step.

Lucy gave her a hard push.

"If I see you walking on green tiles again, you'll be in trouble."

Mrs Higgins came along. She was the Head Teacher.

"You ought to be in your classrooms now," she said. "Hurry up."

Lucy went into the Year 4 room. As she opened the door she turned round and gave Nisba a nasty look.

"Stay off those green tiles," Lucy said. "Daddy-long-legs."

"I've got another question," Nisba said to Mr Martin. "Why can't Year 3 people walk on the green tiles?"

"I don't know," Mr Martin said. "Tell me about it."

Nisba did not want to tell tales. "In the corridor," she said, "there are lots of brown tiles and some yellow tiles and not many green tiles. Someone said only Year 4 people can walk on the green tiles."

"Ah, I see," said Mr Martin. "Well, once upon a time, people used to play hopscotch on the yellow and green tiles, and there were accidents, so the rule is, no jumping. But Year 4 people are taller. They can take bigger steps. There's no rule about that."

"I can take bigger steps too," Nisba said.

Mr Martin looked at her.

"You're a very tall girl, Nisba," he said. "You go ahead and walk where you like."

At lunch-time, Nisba went up the corridor on the green tiles, and into the cloakroom.

Lucy Wells was waiting for her.

"I saw you walking on the green tiles," Lucy said. She had friends with her.

"Mr Martin said I could walk on them," Nisba said. "Mr Martin says I can walk where I like."

"It's nothing to do with him," said one of Lucy's friends. "We say you can't."

"Anyway," Lucy said, "you're a new girl. New girls can only walk on brown tiles. Everyone knows that."

Nisba looked at Lucy and Lucy's friends. None of them was as tall as Nisba. Suddenly she understood. They were angry because she *could* reach the green tiles without jumping, not because she *did*.

Silly little things, Nisba thought. She went out of the cloakroom and stood on a green tile. Someone behind her hooked a foot round her ankle. She lost her balance and fell over, hitting her arm on the step at the bottom of the staircase.

Mrs Higgins came out of the staff room and saw Nisba sitting on the floor. Nisba was trying not to cry. Lucy was pretending that she had just come out of the cloakroom. Lucy's friends began to look at a picture on the wall.

"Lucy and Nisba *again?*" Mrs Higgins said. "I hope you're not fighting."

"I slipped on the tiles," Nisba said.

"Yes, she slipped," said Lucy, and Lucy's friends.

Nisba stood up. She had a big red mark on her arm.

"That will be a nasty bruise," Mrs Higgins said. "You need the Hand of Peace on that. Go to the staff room and say I sent you. The rest of you get your lunch."

Nisba went up the steps to the staff room and knocked on the door.

Miss Shah came out. "Who are you?" she said.

"I'm Nisba," Nisba said. "I'm new. Mrs Higgins says I need the Hand of Peace."

She showed Miss Shah her bruise.

"Come in, then," Miss Shah said. "How did you do that?"

"I slipped and fell on the steps," Nisba said. She followed Miss Shah into the staff room.

All the teachers were sitting in comfy chairs, eating their lunch and drinking coffee. In the corner was a sink, and a draining board, and a little fridge. Miss Shah opened the fridge.

"Will it hurt?" Nisba said, as Miss Shah took something out of the ice box.

"You tell me," Miss Shah said. "It looks as if it hurts already."

"No, not my arm. The Hand of Peace."

Miss Shah laughed. "It's not the Hand of *Peace*, Nisba, it's the Hand of *Peas*.

Someone found out that a good thing for a bruise is to put a packet of frozen peas on it. We've got something even better."

She was holding a white plastic glove, tied at the wrist with string.

"The peas are in the glove," Miss Shah said.

"Go and sit in the front hall for a bit. Hold the glove against your poor arm and it will feel like a nice cool hand."

The front hall was a good place to sit. There were armchairs for visitors, and a piece of carpet, and three tall plants in pots.

Nisba had sat here once before, with Mum, when they came to ask Mrs Higgins if Nisba could go to Farm Lane School.

Nisba took the best chair and held the Hand of Peas against her bruise. It was so cold she could feel it making the swelling go down. It felt like peace, even if it was only frozen peas.

From her chair Nisba could see past the staff room, down the steps and along the corridor.

Mrs Higgins was there, with Mr Keates the caretaker. They were crawling about, poking the floor.

Mrs Higgins did not often crawl about on the floor. She had nice trousers on, too.

"Here's another," Mr Keates said. "Split right across. It's those pipes again."

"One of the little ones tripped just now," Mrs Higgins said.

That's me, Nisba thought. They think I tripped on a loose tile. But I'm not little. That's the trouble.

Mrs Higgins came back up the steps and saw Nisba.

"Better now?" she said.

"Yes, thank you," Nisba said.

"Go and have your lunch, then," Mrs Higgins said. She went into her special room with HEAD TEACHER on the door.

Nisba took the Hand of Peas off her arm. Now her skin was icy cold and the Hand was warm and floppy. She knocked on the door of the staff room. Miss Shah came to take the Hand away.

"I'll put it back in the fridge to get cold for someone else," she said.

Nisba walked down the steps and along the corridor. Now that she was looking for them she could see the split tiles. Some of the green tiles were split, but she stepped on them anyway, because Lucy had said she must not.

She did not really want to walk on green tiles all the time, but Lucy was a bully, and bullies must never be allowed to win.

Then it was Saturday. There was no school for two whole days, so Nisba wore her bangles. But every time she looked at her arm she saw the fading bruise, and thought of Lucy.

Was Lucy a bully? Bullies were supposed to be big and tough. Nisba was bigger than Lucy, but Lucy had friends.

Four little bullies were as bad as one big one.

On Monday it was very cold. As Nisba walked across the playground she thought of the warm floor in the hall where they would sit for assembly.

She hung up her coat in the cloakroom and went into the corridor. Something had happened. Something was different.

It was the floor.

During the weekend Mr Keates had been at work. Nisba remembered how he had crawled on the floor with Mrs Higgins, counting split tiles. He had taken them all away and put new ones down.

The new tiles were grey, and they were all over the place. Some of them were in the hopscotch patterns instead of green tiles or yellow ones. No one could walk down the corridor on only green tiles now, they were too far apart.

Not even Mr Martin would be able to do it, and he was the tallest teacher.

At the end of the corridor by the Year 4 room, people were trying to walk on green tiles. Lucy took a huge step but it was no use, she could not reach.

"Nyah, nyah," Lucy said, when she saw Nisba. "Now you'll have to walk on the brown tiles, Daddy-long-legs."

"No I won't," Nisba said, and she walked all the way down the corridor on the new grey tiles. It was the hardest thing she had ever done and she nearly fell over twice, but she stepped on every grey tile.

Lucy and her friends were growling.

When Nisba got to the end of the corridor they

all started to walk the other way, but no one else could step on all the grey tiles. They had to hop between some of them.

Neesa and Aishe were watching. They went into the Year 3 room and fetched Mr Martin. They knew what Lucy was like. They knew what Lucy had done to Nisba.

"People are jumping in the corridor," Neesa said. "They mustn't do that, must they?"

"No," said Mr Martin, and he came out to see what was going on.

"Here comes Mr Martin. Look out!" said one of Lucy's friends.

Lucy was just starting to jump. She tried to stop but it was too late, and she sat down hard on the floor.

"What's all this?" Mr Martin said. Lucy started to cry.

"Have you hurt yourself?" Mr Martin said.

"I bumped my head," Lucy said. It was not true. She had bumped her bottom but she did not want to say so.

"Go and get the Hand of Peas," Mr Martin said. "If we have any more accidents they will close the school. Now, what are you all doing?"

No one said anything.

"I hear you have been jumping," Mr Martin said. "Were you playing hopscotch? You know that is not allowed."

"I was walking on the grey tiles," Nisba said. "I wasn't jumping."

Lucy came back. She had the Hand of Peas on her head. "I didn't jump," she said. "Not really, I didn't. I just didn't quite walk."

"And I can't quite fly," Mr Martin said. "Jumping is both feet off the ground at once. I know all about how you walk on special tiles, but walking is not jumping. Let's see who can do it. Start at the steps and see how far you get."

One after the other the Year 4 people tried to walk down the corridor, stepping only on the new grey tiles, but no one could do it.

"Now Nisba," Mr Martin said, and Nisba went down the corridor again, stepping on the grey tiles.

"That's not fair," Lucy said. "She's only got a little bit of her foot on some of those tiles."

"It is fair," Aishe said. "Robert only had a tiny bit of his foot on the white tile, but he still broke his arm."

"This could get dangerous," Mr Martin said. "What have you started, Nisba?"

"I'm sorry," Nisba said, but she did not think she had done anything wrong.

"You need not be sorry," Mr Martin said, "but are you always going to walk on the grey tiles?"

"No," Nisba said. "It hurts my legs where they join on. I just wanted to see if I could."

"There," Mr Martin said. "Do you understand? You don't *have* to do something just because you *can*. If Nisba stops walking on the grey tiles, will the rest of you stop trying to?"

They all nodded, but Lucy hissed, "Daddy-long-legs."

"Stop it, Lucy," Mr Martin said. "And do put that horrible Hand back in the fridge. It looks as if someone is trying to pull your head off."

"Nisba can't be a daddy," Neesa said. "She's a girl."

"She'll be a lady, not a daddy," Aishe said.

And Nisba said, "That's right. I'm Lady Long-legs."

EASY PEASY

by SARAH HAYES
illustrated by
JOHN BENDALL-BRUNELLO

Sam wasn't at school when the battered yellow van arrived. He should have been. But he wasn't. He was sitting on the steps outside his flat. The van stopped and a woman got out. She had short purple hair.

The woman opened the back of the van and three silver skittles rolled onto the pavement.

97

Then a tall man in a hat got out. He was holding a baby wearing shoes with bells on them.

Sam jumped down the steps, picked up the skittles and put them back in the van.

The man bowed. "Hold Piglet a minute," he said, and handed Sam the baby. Sam had never held a baby before.

The man took off his hat and tipped out three puffy gold stars and two gold moons. Then he threw them all into the air and caught them one by one. Round his head, through his legs, behind his back went the stars and the moons. "Joe Juggles," the man said. "At your service."

"Dropped it," said the baby. But the stars and moons went on whirling round and round.

The woman with the purple hair put her hand to her mouth and made a noise like someone playing a trumpet.

"Toots, the Human Trumpet," said Joe.

"I'm Sam," said Sam. He took a deep breath. "Sam Small."

Joe Juggles didn't laugh. He didn't even smile. He caught the stars and moons in his hat and said, "Now that is a very useful name."

"Not if you're the smallest boy in the school," said Sam.

Joe sat down on the top step and took Piglet onto his knee.

Sam jumped up the steps, all four of them at once.

"Do that again," said Toots.

"Easy peasy," said Sam. He jumped down and then back up. Toots nodded but she didn't say anything. So Sam sat down next to Joe and told him about being the smallest boy in the school. It was trouble. It was three kinds of trouble.

Trouble with the dinner ladies.

Trouble with the big girls.

Trouble with horrible Beany Bennett.

When Sam had finished, Joe stood up. "What do you think, Toots?" he said.

Toots didn't reply. Instead she stood on her head.

"Don't worry," said Joe. "Just be quiet and wait."

Sam waited. And waited. And then it came. Toots's lips were moving, but it wasn't Toots's voice. It wasn't the Human Trumpet either. This is what it said:

> *When long becomes short*
> *And small becomes tall,*
> *No one will trouble*
> *Amazing Sam Small.*

"It's a message," said Joe. "You don't have to do a thing."

Toots turned the right way up and said, "Come and see us tomorrow, Sam, when we're unpacked. It's not very far. Just up the stairs."

And that was the day that Joe Juggles, Toots the Human Trumpet and Baby Piglet moved into the upstairs flat – the day things began to change for Sam Small.

Next morning Sam took a cake upstairs.

The door was slightly open, but Sam didn't know whether to go in. Then he saw Joe.

Joe took the cake and picked up a stick. Then he spun the plate on the top of the stick and put the bottom of the stick on his nose.

Toots came in. "It's a big mistake to juggle cake," she said.

Joe stepped backwards and bumped into a blow-up gorilla.

The plate flew off the stick.

Sam jumped and caught the plate as it came down. But the cake slid off and landed on his head.

Toots scooped off a lump.

Joe helped himself to a bit of cake.

Sam just stood there. It felt funny having people eating off the top of your head.

"Sam Small, the Human Plate," Sam said, and they all got the giggles. A drip of chocolate reached the corner of Sam's mouth. He licked it off.

Joe unhooked a giant wooden spoon from the wall and Toots fetched a teaspoon.

They were scraping the last of the cake off Sam's head when Piglet staggered in. She was holding a huge rabbit.

"Meet Snowflake," said Joe. "A conjuror gave her to us. She got too big for his hat."

The baby and the rabbit sat down very suddenly. "Dropped it," said Piglet.

The huge pile of fluff hopped towards Sam. Then it stood on its hind legs and nibbled the chocolate in his hair.

Toots said that was Snowflake's way of saying that Sam needed a hair-wash.

Usually Sam hated having his hair washed. But this time it was all right.

Joe filled a big china bowl with warm water and Sam knelt on the rug. Toots blew bubbles through her fingers and Piglet splashed water everywhere. The drying was all right too, because

they used Snowflake's heavy-duty hairdryer. But as
it dried, Sam's hair got curlier and curlier and
more and more knotted.

Sam looked at the tangled mess in the mirror
and he made a decision. "Could you cut my hair?"
he said.

"Sure," said Joe.

"If your mum doesn't mind," added Toots.

Sam's mum wasn't very happy, but in the end
she agreed.

And so Joe did it, with his special clippers and
a Grade Three attachment.

When he had finished, Sam looked completely different. He felt different too, sort of light and bouncy.

For the rest of the day Sam and his mum kept running their hands over the soft fuzz which now covered his head.

When he was in bed Sam realized that the first part of his message had come true.

> *When long becomes short*
> *And small becomes tall,*
> *No one will trouble*
> *Amazing Sam Small.*

His hair had been long. And now it was short.
But what about the rest of the message?

106

Sam was still in his pyjamas when Toots rang the bell next morning.

"Time to go to work," she said. "We'll collect you in five minutes. And it's OK with your mum. We checked last night."

Sam sat in the back of the van with Joe and Piglet, and Toots drove. The van had all sorts of stuff clipped to the sides.

After a long time they stopped in a square with cafés and stalls all round it. On the far side was a big building with pillars. Something black was stuck between two of the pillars, almost at the top.

As they got closer Sam could see that the black thing was a man braced between the pillars. By moving one hand and then one foot and then another hand and another foot he was slowly climbing up the pillars. It looked very dangerous.

There were only a few people watching Fly, but Joe said it was early yet. You had to be there early to get a good pitch. Sam helped unload the van.

Fly climbed down and came over to say hello. Sam thought he looked pretty silly. But Piglet loved him.

While Joe set up the pitch, Fly played with Piglet, and Toots and Sam went off to the park to practise. First they did this:

And then this:

And then this, which was a lot harder:

Toots said that was called a flic-flac and not many people could do it. "You're a born tumbler, Sam," she said. "You've got natural bounce."

When they got back to the square, there were loads of people there. Toots lifted Sam up so he could see over the crowd round their pitch. Joe was riding a unicycle and juggling with a watch, a grapefruit and a baseball cap.

Sam and Toots squeezed through to the front – Joe was still juggling. Toots walked round the ring on her hands and did a bit of Human Trumpeting.

People clapped. Then Toots pinched her nose and said in a loudspeaker voice:

Three people from the audience came into the ring and Joe gave them back their things. Then he picked up Piglet and went round with a hat and most people put money in it. When he got to Sam, Joe winked at him and whispered, "Picnic time."

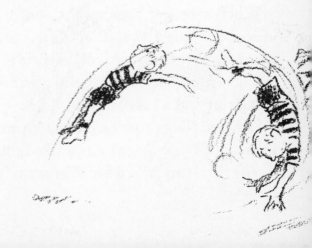

Then he emptied the hat into a lock-up box in his suitcase, and Toots said, "That's it, folks," and the crowd went off to look at someone else's act.

Sam didn't eat much picnic. He was too nervous. Because...

In the afternoon, after a bit of practising, a new act joined Joe Juggles and Toots the Human Trumpet.

At the end of the performance, just before the hat went round, Toots said in her loudspeaker voice:

"And now, for his first public appearance, will you welcome an exciting new tumbler. Please put your hands together for the boy with natural bounce... Sam Small!" Toots did a drum roll and Sam flic-flacked across the ring.

Then Toots walked round on her hands and Sam cartwheeled and Joe cycled round on the unicycle.

The best came last. Toots did a really slow drum roll, and Joe leant down from the unicycle and caught hold of Sam's hands. Sam bounced and Joe lifted. And then he was standing on Joe's shoulders. Round and round the ring they went. People roared and whistled and clapped.

Then Sam jumped down and took the hat round. He collected loads. Joe put it with the rest in the lock-up box in the suitcase.

It was the best day of Sam's life. And he got paid!

When they were driving home Sam remembered his message.

When long becomes short
And small becomes tall,
No one will trouble
Amazing Sam Small.

Another bit of the message had come true. Riding round on Joe's shoulders on the unicycle, Sam Small really had become tall.

Then he remembered something else. Tomorrow was Monday. And that meant school. A whole week of it.

Dinner break was always the worst. They were all there — the dinner ladies, the big girls and horrible Beany Bennett. Three kinds of trouble. Sam dawdled about as long as he could, but in the end he had to go out into the playground.

Usually the dinner ladies called him back to pinch his cheek and ruffle his curls. But today he didn't have any curls to ruffle. And today the dinner ladies let him go past.

Sam put his head down and walked towards the mound. That way he might miss the big girls. They said the mound was only for little kids. But in the playground the big girls were waiting for Sam. And they didn't want to ruffle his curls.

They wanted to pick him up and feel his Grade Three haircut. They thought it was sweet! The biggest of the big girls tried to lift him up, but Sam dived out of her arms into a forward flip. He followed this with two perfect cartwheels and three flic-flacs. The big girls clapped.

"Do it again, Sam!" they shouted.

Sam did it again. Lots of people clapped this time.

A loudspeaker voice boomed across the playground:

"And now will you welcome the boy with natural bounce... Amazing Sam Small."

And there was Toots, standing with Joe and Piglet on the other side of the playground wall.

Sam grinned and waved. Everyone clapped again.

But then, from round the back of the boiler shed, came Beany Bennett. When he saw Sam he stopped and stared.

Everyone began to say it. "Samantha Small, Samantha Small, Samantha Small's not very tall."

Sam took a deep breath, bent his knees and began to flic-flac towards Beany Bennett. One ... two ... three ... four ... five flic-flacs.

When he reached Beany, Sam stared straight into his horrible little eyes.

"Hold out your hands," Sam said. Beany was so surprised that he held out his hands without thinking.

Sam took hold of Beany's hands. "Lift when I say lift," said Sam.

Beany was so surprised that he nodded.

Sam bounced and Beany lifted.

Now Sam stood on Beany's shoulders.

"Walk!" said Sam.

Beany was so surprised that he walked.

A slow drum roll came from the other side of the playground wall. Round and round the playground they walked. Everyone roared and stamped and whistled and clapped.

Then Beany began to stagger so Sam jumped down and whispered, "Bow!" and they both bowed.

"Blimey," said Beany Bennett. And he actually grinned at Sam. Sam grinned back.

The loudspeaker voice boomed:

"Will you welcome the exciting new double act — Big Beany Bennett and Amazing Sam Small."

There was more clapping and then the voice changed:

When long becomes short
And small becomes tall,
No one will trouble
Amazing Sam Small.

And no one ever did.

THERE'S MORE TO A BANANA

by RITA PHILLIPS MITCHELL
illustrated by PAUL HOWARD

"This term I want you to do a project on tropical fruits," Mr Williams announced to the class when we came back from holiday.

"Great!" we cried.

"Easy peasy," said Sammy.

"That may be so, Sam," said Mr Williams. "But don't forget that presentation is important. I want your best writing along with your best drawings, photos and anything else you can think of."

Mr Williams left us to talk among ourselves for a few minutes.

"I'll do one of the citrus fruits," said my friend Elena.

"That's a whole lot of fruits to choose from," I said.

"Well, I don't like lemons and limes." Elena made an awful face. "So that only leaves oranges and grapefruit, right?"

"I'll do guavas," said Jenny Silvers, who sat
behind me. She had a voice which squeaked in
your ears.

"Guavas!" cried Sammy. "They're cow food and they have a pongy smell."

"Don't be silly," said Jenny. "Next you'll be telling me that cows eat guava jelly." Cries of *yum-yum* rippled through the class.

"I'll do mangoes," said David Young. "Because I know a lot about them."

"No! I want to do mangoes," I cried.

"I said it first, so there!" said David.

Several other people began to shout that they wanted to do mangoes. I shook my head and put my hands over my ears. Then Joel, who'd chosen mangoes too, decided to switch to breadfruit.

"That's not a fruit. Whoever heard of a fruit you have to boil, fry or bake before you can eat it? It's more like bread plus fruit," said Sammy grinning wildly. "Get it?"

Everybody started to laugh. Mr Williams cleared his throat. The class went quiet.

"Enough!" he said sharply. "I see I shall have to help you to choose your fruits. But not now. Let's get on with the next lesson first."

We settled down and forgot about the project until hometime. On our way out, Mr Williams asked each of us to pick a piece of paper from a tin on his table. Each piece of paper had the name of a fruit written on it.

"Bananas!" I read when I unfolded mine. "Of all the fruits in the world I had to get bananas!" Suddenly the project didn't seem like such a good idea after all.

"It's not fair," I said when I met up with Flora outside.

"What's wrong?" Flora asked.

"A rotten project on rotten bananas," I said. "That's what's wrong."

"Why? I don't understand," said Flora.

"I wanted to do mangoes. I had the whole thing planned," I said. "But David Young got mangoes and I picked the paper with bananas on it."

"Swap with David then," said Flora.

"He wouldn't. He's real mean and a creep," I said. "What do I know about bananas anyway?"

"I guess as much as you know about mangoes," said Flora. "Just because you've got seventy-three mango seeds in your collection, doesn't mean you know more about mangoes than bananas. Besides, you like bananas a lot, right?"

"Not any more, I don't," I said.

"Since when?" Flora asked.

"Since I've got to do a project on them," I said.

"I'll tell you what," said Flora. "Why don't you draw pictures of all kinds of bananas and fill up your book with them: green and ripe, big and small, jungle bananas and even whole bunches?"

"Oh yes! And what shall I write about the pictures?" I said.

"Plenty," went on Flora. "Under a baby banana you can write 'Don't eat me until I grow up'. And under a jungle banana ... 'I'm wild'."

"Very funny," I said. "You don't know how to be helpful, that's your problem."

"Yes I do," said Flora. "But only when you really really need it."

I glared at her.

We arrived home, still arguing. My father took one look at me and said jokingly, "Oh, Grandma! What a long face you've got today!"

"As long as a banana," Flora said, laughing at her own joke.

"Shut up," I hissed.

"Shush!" said my father. "What's the problem?"

"BANANAS!" I groaned, and I explained about the project.

"Soooooooooo," he said. "Where's the problem?"

"The problem is I really, really wanted to do mangoes."

"Sometimes we have to do things we don't like. That's a fact of life," said my father. "And another fact is, when working on a project you must always start with what you know. Read up on what you don't know or ask those who do."

"Like me," said Flora.

"You! What can *you* tell me?" I said.

"Lots. The banana is a very soft, fleshy fruit, but it doesn't have lashings of juice like mangoes and oranges. When it's ripe even a baby can peel it, but when it's green you need a knife to get the skin off. You can't eat a green banana unless you cook it first. You can make banana chips, dumplings and flour. The banana is a longish fruit, as long as—"

"Stop, Flora!" my father said, laughing.

I said nothing. I couldn't believe Flora knew so much about bananas.

All that weekend I worried and fussed about my project. I told everyone who came to the house about it, and everyone had something to say.

My Uncle Bill sang, "Yes, we have no bananas. We have no bananas today."

"Look at me. I'm as fit as a flea," said my grandmother twirling round. "That's because I'm a banana-a-day person. I eat them raw. I eat them cooked. But the best dish for me is salted mackerel with boiled green bananas. Believe me child, there's more to that fruit than meets the eye."

On Sunday I wrote down everything I had learnt. Afterwards I added a little more each day.

The next Friday afternoon the class read out their first reports. David talked on and on about mangoes. I could have bopped him. Elena had so much to say about oranges that Mr Williams told her to leave some of it for next week. Gary Meddows knew a lot of interesting facts about watermelons, but nobody was surprised. His father grew them in his back garden. It was covered in miles of tangled watermelon vines. They ran along the ground like crazy, turning corners and twisting themselves around anything that got in their way. When Gary finished reading, the whole class clapped. Next Sisty read her report on the sapodilla.

"Very interesting, Sisty," said Mr Williams looking at his watch. "We have time for one more. Melanie, shall we have bananas today?"

I looked at my book. I sighed. Part of the fun of doing a project is seeing who can find the most exciting title. Elena had "Oranges Are Best". David Young's was "A Bucketful of Mangoes", while Sisty called hers "Gummy-gummy Sapodillas". I only had one word. In a very thin voice I read out "Bananas". Everybody sniggered. I pretended I didn't care and read on. "The banana is a longish fruit and some are curved and look like tiny boomerangs. When ripe the banana is yellow, soft and fleshy, but it doesn't have lashings of juice like oranges and mangoes. And even a baby can peel the skin off. But oh boy! When it's green the skin is stuck on so hard you have to use a knife to cut it away. You can boil green bananas or make chips or dumplings from them and even flour for porridge—"

"What about bananas with brown spots on them?" cried somebody.

"I call those Dalmatian bananas," said Sammy, grinning. "Get it?"

"Not funny," said Jenny Silvers in her squeaky voice. And everybody started to giggle.

"Carry on, Melanie," said Mr Williams.

"Bananas grow in hot countries like the West Indies, Ecuador, Mexico, Belize, Australia, the Philippines and hundreds of other places. They like a hot climate but if the weather gets too hot the leaves of the plant shrivel up. My grandma says that there's more to a banana than meets the eye, but I don't know what she means."

"Good, Melanie," said Mr Williams. "I won't spoil it by explaining what your gran means. You'll find out for yourself soon enough."

That evening my father said, "Reading something interesting, Mel?"

"Not really," I said. "It's a book on bananas I got from Mr Williams."

"Have you learnt anything new?" he asked, looking over my shoulder.

"Yes," I said. "You didn't tell me that bananas have names. It says so in this book."

"Sometimes it's more fun to find out things for yourself," my father said. "The names are beautiful, don't you think? Robusta, Lacatan, Gros Michel, Giant Cavendish, Dwarf Cavendish, Valery. And there's the Mons Mari species in Australia. Anyway, how did you get on at school today?"

"All right, I suppose," I said glumly.

"We've got a little surprise to cheer you up," said my father. "I've arranged for us to visit my friend's banana plantation next weekend."

I felt better already. I couldn't help giving him a tiny smile. My father smiled back. "That's more like it," he said.

Early Saturday morning we drove to Manuel's banana plantation. We got out of the pick-up truck and a huge, noisy grey dog bounded towards us. Flora and I tucked ourselves between Poppa and Momma. My father patted the dog and she stopped barking and started to wag her tail.

"My friends," cried Manuel from the verandah, "you've made it, I see."

"Wouldn't have missed it for the world," said my father.

Then Manuel looked down at Flora and me. He grinned. I saw his gold tooth glistening in the sunlight.

"Which of you girls would like to be a banana expert then?" he asked.

"Me," I said. "I've got to do a project."

"Yes," said Flora, "and she wants you to tell her lots and lots so she can get good marks."

"I'll do my best," smiled Manuel.

The farm door opened in a hurry. Manuel's wife, Theresa, came rushing out onto the verandah.

"Hola mis amigos," she cried, shaking my father's hand. Then she and my mother wrapped their arms around each other, talking all the while. Theresa spoke Spanish and a little English. My mother spoke English dotted with a Spanish word here and there. It sounded funny but they seemed to understand each other very well.

A few minutes later Theresa turned to us.

"Hola Melanie and Flora," she said. "Something to drink, yes?"

Before we could answer she had disappeared

into the house, and soon we were holding a glass in one hand and a slice of cake in the other.

"Banana and cinnamon, mmmmmm!" I said, sipping the frothy drink.

"Can I have your cake, Mel?" teased Flora. "You don't like bananas any more, remember?"

"This is different," I said, gulping down my drink to the last drop and biting into the cake, which was delicious. Manuel stood up. He slapped a black hat on his head and eased the strap under his chin.

"Let's go," he said, walking down the steps. My father, Flora and I followed him. My mother stayed with Theresa. They told us they had a lot of catching up to do.

The plantation was right behind the farmhouse. Everywhere we looked were rows and rows and rows of banana plants.

"Owee!" squealed Flora. "They're like an army of soldiers standing still."

My father and Manuel laughed. The plants grew in orderly straight lines with equal space between them. Every plant had one bunch of very green bananas hanging on it. The banana leaves were broad and long. They were like green umbrellas shading the bananas from the hot sun. We walked between the rows of plants where it was shady and cool.

"Look, I'm nearly as tall as this tree," said Flora, standing under a huge bunch of bananas.

"It's not a tree, it's a plant," corrected Manuel.

"When is a tree not a tree?" my father shouted. He had stopped to take pictures and was coming to join us again, adjusting his camera strap over his shoulder.

"When I can't climb it," Flora shouted back.

Manuel laughed. "Very clever."

"When the lumberjack cries TIMBER!" said my father.

"You read too many comics my friend," said Manuel. "What do you think, Melanie?"

"When it's a plant," I said.

"Very witty, but in order to get full marks, tell me what you notice about this," said Manuel, pointing at a stem.

"It's much softer than the trunk of a tree," said Flora, wrapping her arms around it.

"And there's no bark and no woody part," I said. "And no lumberjack would want to chop it down because there's no timber, right?"

"Go to the top of the class," said my father.

What a lot I'm learning already! I thought to myself as I sat on a stump and wrote up my notes.

"Now," said Manuel, "how about a little maths?"

"What's maths got to do with bananas?" I asked.

"Plenty," said Manuel. "I'm nearly two metres tall. Can you guess how big this plant is?"

"Three metres," shouted Flora.

"Taller," I said.

"Good," said Manuel. "This plant is five metres, but I've some that are shorter too. Now take a plant each and count the number of leaves."

My father had to help Flora because the leaves kept swaying about in the breeze. I counted seventy. Flora and my father counted sixty on theirs.

"Good," said Manuel. "There are sixty to seventy leaves on each plant. And I'll tell you something else: each week a banana plant grows one leaf."

"Really? So it took seventy weeks to grow all the leaves on my plant," I said.

"Great guns! That was quick," said Manuel.

"I'm quick at counting too," said Flora.

"Of course you are," said my father.

Manuel pulled back the leaves from a bunch of bananas. "Do you notice anything strange about how the bunch hangs?"

My father bent down, his hands almost touching the ground. I knew he was giving us a clue.

"The bunch grows downwards on the plant," I cried.

"Correct," said Manuel. "And what about the bananas?"

"They grow upwards."

"That's funny," said Flora, "the bunch grows downwards and the bananas grow upwards."

Then Manuel told us to count the number of bananas on a hand. A hand is really another name for a cluster of bananas. We counted fifteen. Manuel told us that a good bunch always has eight or nine hands.

"If bananas have hands then hands should have fingers, right?" said Flora, trying to be funny.

"Actually, a single banana *is* called a finger," said Manuel.

"See! I'm right!" Flora grinned.

"I think it's time for a little diversion," said Manuel, winking at my father. "Ready, girls?" We nodded. We walked to a clearing where the earth was dry and the grass grew in tufts. Manuel kept looking at the ground, searching for something with his foot. Suddenly he pulled up a handful of grass. We saw a hole so small even Flora's fist couldn't fit in it. Manuel tapped around it with his feet. My father joined him. Flora and I stood well back. Watching them reminded me of the

Mexican hat dance, where dancers circle round a hat with their hands behind their backs.

"There it is!" cried Manuel suddenly. "Isn't she a beauty?"

Flora and I stared at the black, velvety, hairy tarantula. It came a little way out of the hole. I jumped back. Flora screamed and the tarantula scarpered back into the hole.

"Tarantulas aren't interested in us," said Manuel. "They much prefer to hide in a bunch of bananas and travel to foreign countries free of charge."

We all laughed except Flora. She ran off.

The other end of the plantation was busy and noisy. Some workers were chopping down bunches of bananas with sharp machetes. Others were loading up trucks and shouting orders at each other.

"There are only green bananas here," I said. "Why is that?"

"We only send green bananas abroad," said Manuel. "Ripe bananas would be spoilt by the end of their journey."

"Phew!" I said. "What a lot there is to know about bananas! My book is nearly full."

On our way back to the house a truck with "Cavendish" written on the side roared past us.

"Ah! Cavendish," I said. "Do you grow Robusta, Lacatan and Gros Michel too?"

"She is a little expert on the quiet," Manuel told my father. My father gave me a huge smile.

"I'll never ever forget today, Manuel," I said. "Thank you very much."

I spent most of Sunday designing my book. It was in the shape of a huge banana. The front cover was crayoned in yellow and the back in green. On each page I wrote the name of a species of banana. Afterwards I drew some pictures and cut out others from a *National Geographic* magazine to make a collage of a plantation. I had so much to write, it took the whole week to finish it.

"Don't forget to leave enough space for my wonderful photos," smiled my father.

Two weeks later Mr Williams asked us to show our projects to the class. Soon everybody was busy piling the display tables with fruits, leaves, seeds, pictures and posters. There were cakes, sweets and fruit preserves.

"It's like harvest time," said Sammy, and everyone agreed.

Each day five people read out their projects and it took a week before everyone had had a turn. I was hoping mine would be the best, but everyone else had worked very hard too. My turn came on the last day.

"I shall leave the title to the end," I told the class.

Then I held up my book to show them the front and back covers.

"Brilliant!" they cried.

I didn't need to read out my work because I remembered most of what I had written. I just showed the pictures and talked as I turned the pages.

At the end I said, "Although I have learnt so much about the banana, there is a whole lot more I don't know. And that's why I have called my project 'There's More to a Banana than Meets the Eye'."

"Well done, Melanie," said Mr Williams. "In fact I have never seen the whole class work so hard on a project before."

"Well sir," said Sammy, "you could say that there is more to *us* than meets the eye, right?"

The whole class laughed, even Mr Williams.

THE

END

Acknowledgements

"Brian Big Head" from *Big Head*
Text © 1999 Jean Ure Illustrations © 1999 Mike Gordon

"Ten Past Two" from *In Crack Willow Wood*
Text © 1995 Sam McBratney Illustrations © 1995 Ivan Bates

"The Super-doodle Plan" from *Jackson's Juniors*
Text © 1993 Vivian French Illustrations © 1993 Thelma Lambert

Posh Watson
Text © 1995 Gillian Cross Illustrations © 1995 Mike Gordon

"Magic in the Air" from *Carrie Climbs a Mountain*
Text © 1993 June Crebbin Illustrations © 1993 Thelma Lambert

Lady Long-legs
Text © 1999 Jan Mark Illustrations © 1999 Paul Howard

Easy Peasy
Text © 1994 Sarah Hayes Illustrations © 1994 John Bendall-Brunello

There's More to a Banana
Text © 1999 Rita Phillips Mitchell Illustrations © 1999 Paul Howard